J.A

T

W24
LC-6/1/19

AJI 9/11/00
CC-8

DISCARD

DATE DUE

F   7-3-78

Ballard
   The sheriff of Tombstone

no longer merely employer and employee.

Jess threw herself into his arms, knowing that here she had found a true sanctuary.

THE END

CUCKOO IN THE NEST

Joyce Johnson

On his deathbed, reclusive million-aire Sir Harry Trevain asks his beloved granddaughter, Daisy, to restore harmony to their fractured family. But as the Trevain family gathers for Sir Harry's funeral, tensions are already surfacing. Then, at the funeral, a handsome stranger arrives from America claiming to be Sir Harry's grandson. The family is outraged, but Daisy, true to her promise to her grandfather, wel-comes the stranger to Pencreek and finds herself irresistibly drawn to Ben Trevain . . .

'I'LL BE THERE FOR YOU'

Chrissie Loveday

Amy returns home to find the house deserted and her father mysteriously absent. Her oldest friend Greg rallies round and they begin their mission to find her father. Had her father planned some sort of surprise holiday for her? Or was there a sinister purpose behind the mysterious phone calls? Mystery, adventure, possible danger and a trip to Southern Spain follow. But how could they enjoy the beautiful settings with such threats hanging over them?

JANE I'M-STILL-SINGLE JONES

Joan Reeves

Despite her ownership of a successful business in New York, Jane Louise Jones is nervous about her impending high school reunion in Vernon, Louisiana. There she must wear a badge emblazoned with her unmarried status, which Morgan Sherwood might see. Unbelievably handsome and now rich, Morgan had broken her heart in the senior year. Meanwhile, Morgan plans to make her fall in love with him all over again, he's never forgotten their passionate kisses — and now he wants more . . .

THE BAKER'S APPRENTICE

Valerie Holmes

Molly Mason dreams of escaping from the suffocating existence of life with her stepmother, Mrs Cecily Creswell and her daughter Juniper. She plans to make her escape by becoming an apprentice to her friend the local baker, Alice Arndale. However, when Juniper's fiancé Lt. Cherry, a war hero, returns home early, he arrives with Mr Julian Creswell, a missing soldier, presumed dead — and Julian brings with him suspicions of murder, mystery and the key to Molly's heart . . .

MOONLIGHT AND SHADOW

Jasmina Svenne

When Andrew Melbury impulsively marries Leah Hancock, his grandmother's companion, he is aware they barely know each other. But all such considerations seem irrelevant in the face of their love. It is only after a potentially fatal encounter on a moonlit road in Sherwood Forest that Andrew begins to question why Leah has always been so reticent about her past. What secrets has she been keeping from him? And are both their lives in danger?

WALTER SPEAZLEBUD

DAVID DONOHUE

Illustrated by
The Cartoon Saloon

THE O'BRIEN PRESS
DUBLIN

First published 2002 by The O'Brien Press Ltd,
12 Terenure Road East, Rathgar, Dublin 6, Ireland.
Tel: +353 1 4923333; Fax: +353 1 4922777
E-mail: books@obrien.ie
Website: www.obrien.ie
Reprinted 2002, 2008.

ISBN: 978-0-86278-762-2

British Library Cataloguing-in-Publication Data
Donohue, David
Walter Speazlebud
1.Children's stories
I.Title
823.9'2[J]

3 4 5 6 7 8 9 10
08 09 10 11

The O'Brien Press receives
assistance from

Editing, typesetting, layout and design: The O'Brien Press Ltd
Illustrations: The Cartoon Saloon
Printing: Cox & Wyman Ltd

Dedication

For Sara, Heather and Eva;
Eve, Jordan, Elijah and John;
Cjartan, Conor and Robyn;
Levon and Lulu.

My thanks to:

Herbie Brennan, Jacquie Burgess, Kirsten Sheridan,
Denis, Paul Hewson, Barbara Galavan, Frank
Golden, Eve Golden Woods, Nick Kelly,
Douglas Gresham, Mark Kilroy, Trish
Mc Adam, Luis and Karen, Berne Kiely and
Amelia Caulfield, Geraldine Bigelow,
and to my editor Susan Houlden.
A special 'thank you' to Bernard
Loughlin and Mary Loughlin
and to all the current staff
at the Tyrone Guthrie Centre
in Monaghan.

Contents

1

Trouble at School

'What the heck is a moon-pet-doctor?' yelled Mr Strong, the school teacher. He had just caught Walter Speazlebud staring out the window during class and had asked him what he was thinking about.

Walter's big, green, happy eyes drifted, once again, out the classroom window and towards the heavens, before he replied: 'A moon-pet-doctor, sir? Oh, that's a person who helps pets – say, for instance, cats – to adjust to the idea of living on the moon. He gets them used to floating, and no mice, that sort of thing.'

Mr Strong pounded his fist on the desk, which was always covered in a thick, black, felt material. 'Come back to Earth, you curly-headed nincompoop. Nobody lives on the moon,' he barked.

'Oh, but they will some day, sir,' replied Walter. 'And when they do, a moon-pet-doctor will be a very busy man. Did you never think of going to the moon yourself, Mr Strong?' he continued, with a look of genuine curiosity.

The class laughed nervously as they knew that Mr Strong had absolutely no imagination or sense of humour.

Mr Strong's face twisted with anger and a blood-red flush entered his cheeks. Beads of sweat formed on his nose and chin, and dripped like a leaky tap onto the classroom floor.

'Come up here, now!' he screamed at Walter.

'Why, sir?' protested Walter innocently.

'For staring into space during spelling lessons, and for being a cheeky pup.'

'I was only thinking, sir.'

'There'll be no thinking in my class,' replied Mr Strong. 'And let this be a lesson to you all.'

Mr Strong pointed to the tall, tubular

metal stool which stood between his desk
and the blackboard. 'Stand on the stool,
Walter, and face the class.'

Walter walked, like a condemned man,
towards the stool. As he did, he accidentally brushed against the material covering
the desk. It shifted slightly.

'Oops,' said Walter, as he went to
straighten it.

'Don't touch my desk. Don't ANYBODY
EVER touch my desk.'

'Why is your desk always covered, sir?'
asked Walter, who had noticed how Mr
Strong always stuck close to his desk, as if
it had magnetic powers.

'Don't ask questions. Won't need
answers. Now get up on the stool. NOW!'

Mr Strong always made sure that the
legs were well greased with the slimiest
goose-fat to make climbing the stool almost
impossible. He stood with his arms crossed,
like an army general, and smiled as Walter
slithered and slipped, trying desperately to
climb up onto the stool. The stool toppled

over and Walter landed on his bottom. His best friend, Levon Allen, looked away – he couldn't bear to watch. After several failed attempts, Walter stood still, concentrated deeply, took one well-judged leap and finally made it onto the stool, with his curly red hair sticking to his sweating, freckled face. His thin body trembled as he faced the class, balancing with all his might.

'Spell **antelope**,' said Mr Strong.

'**E-p-o-l-e-t-n-a**,' replied Walter.

The class remained silent except for Danny Biggles, the school bully, who giggled and guffawed from the back of the room.

'**Catastrophe**,' said Mr Strong.

'**E-h-p-o-r-t-s-a-t-a-c**,' mumbled Walter, trying like mad not to fall off the stool.

No, Walter was not good at spelling – at least spelling forwards. As for spelling backwards, he was a king, and when Mr Strong asked him to spell **concentration**, he, once again, rattled off the perfect backwards spelling: '**N-o-i-t-a-r-t-n-e-c-n-o-c**.'

Mr Strong sneered at the awfulness of Walter's spelling while the class, except for Danny Biggles, who was still chuckling to himself, remained silent.

The boys were fascinated by Walter's gift and they loved when he pronounced their names backwards: Walter's friend **Levon Allen** became **Novel Nella**. **Aron Kelly** became **Nora Yllek, Danny Biggles** became **Ynnad Selggib** (although the boys never called him Ynnad Selggib to his face, as he was very likely to puncture your bicycle tyre or give you a black eye) and **Mr Strong**, the teacher they all hated, became **Mr Gnorts**. They loved to invent sayings like, 'I see warts on **Mr Gnorts**,' or '**Mr Gnorts, Mr Gnorts,** like a skunk he smells, like a pig he snorts.'

'I see, Speazlebud,' said Mr Strong, nodding his head and scratching his chin. 'You can imagine being a pet-doctor on the moon, but you can't spell a few simple little words. Well, I do hope that the class will take note of what happens to a boy who dreams and thinks too much. Have you any more dreams that you would like to share with the class?'

'Yes,' said Walter, 'to appear on Sam Silver's TV show spelling backwards, so that my grandfather can see me.'

Mr Strong's face got redder and redder. 'Backwards spelling is wrong spelling,' he shouted at Walter. 'It's not spelling at all, you stupid little red-headed sparrowbrain. Indeed, Walter,' he muttered, as he stopped pacing and stood directly in front of Walter, 'you are just like your grandfather – a dreamer, away with the fairies, head in the clouds.'

Grandad Speazlebud was Walter's favourite person in the world. He could never let *anybody* make fun of him, least of all Mr Strong. He pretended to lose his balance and, with a careful aim, toppled off the stool, grabbing Mr Strong's new blue shirt which tore all the way down to his waist, just like a rotten old rag.

'Sorry,' said Walter. 'I lost my balance.'

The classroom erupted in laughter to see Mr Strong's hairy belly, bloated from too much cider and pig's trotters, hanging out, over his belt, like a bulging sack of potatoes. The school bell rang and Walter ran out the door and down the hall, out the school gates and down the street, until he was a safe distance from school.

2

Wild Tales

Like Walter, Grandad Speazlebud was good at spelling backwards.

'What's my name backwards?' Walter loved to ask his grandad when he was very little.

'**Retlaw Dubelzaeps**,' his grandad would say.

'And what's a **spider**?'

'A **redips**.'

'And a **monkey**?'

'A **yeknom**, of course.'

'And a **giraffe**?'

'An **effarig**.'

'And a **turkey**?'

'A **yekrut**,' Grandad would reply.

Walter loved Grandad Speazlebud's crazy spelling, but before long he, too, knew that a **boy** was a **yob**, a **cat** was a **tac**, and an **alligator** was a **rotagilla**. He soon discovered that while normal spelling was very difficult, he could spell any word backwards, perfectly, just as quickly as anybody else could spell it forwards.

Walter's grandad was a great storyteller, and most of his stories were about something or other going backwards. Walter wasn't sure if he believed them or not, but he thought they were brilliant fun.

Sometimes, when Grandad told these fantastic stories, he would reverse around the room, in his motorised wheelchair. Walter stood in the middle of the floor, following his spinning grandad with his eyes, getting dizzier and dizzier as the story unfolded.

Walter's favourite story was the one about the little deer. When Grandad told this particular story he always started with a serious tone. He would take Walter's hand, look around to make sure nobody else was listening and, with a gentle voice, begin:

'One day I was on the way home from an afternoon's fishing when I saw a baby deer running out of the woods and on to the road. I knew that the deer, which was puffing and panting in the middle of the road, did not see the car coming towards her.'

Then, with a mischievous glint in his eye, Grandad would stare across the room at the imaginary deer and put his hands around his mouth to form a 'megaphone'. 'Get out of the way, Rudolf!' Grandad would shout at the top of his voice. 'There's a motorised vehicle coming.'

Sometimes, when he told the story, Grandad picked up a banana, or a plum, and fired it at the 'deer' to scare him off. Once a plum went sailing out the window and hit the postman on the nose.

'But the deer ignored me,' Grandad would continue. 'Then, without thinking, I shouted the word "deer" backwards, again and again. **Reed! Reed! Reed!**' Grandad would shout at the top of his voice.

artist, and her big, bright, garish paintings hung all over the house. Walter thought that they should be looked at only while wearing sunglasses. However, he never had to suffer the paintings for too long as, one by one, they were sold to people of odd taste, bringing in enough money to feed the three of them.

Walter was still in a daydream, thinking about his talk with Grandad, when he heard his dad's voice. 'You're a million miles away, **Retlaw**,' Harry said, as he put his hand on Walter's shoulder.

'Dad,' Walter asked, 'if Grandad can spell backwards and I can spell backwards, why can't you?'

'Well,' said Harry, 'sometimes gifts can skip a generation. That's why you're not an inventor like me.'

'Oh,' said Walter, looking slightly worried, 'does that mean that when I grow up and have kids they might turn out to be inventors?'

'I'm afraid so, son,' Harry chuckled.

'And Dad,' Walter continued, 'Can Grandad *really* make things go backwards? He says he has a special power called **Noitanigami**.'

Harry Speazlebud crouched down and placed his hands on Walter's shoulders. 'Walter,' he said, 'your grandad believes that the stories he tells you are true. Doctor Kilroy calls them delusions – this means that Grandad imagines things that never happened. He slips between this world and the world of fantasy just like a child. The best thing to do, Walter, is to smile and agree with him.'

Walter didn't like one little bit the idea of his grandfather going funny in the head. Had Grandad ever really known Mr Strong? he now asked himself. Had Grandad actually made the Condor Chair himself and now imagined that it had been made by Mr Strong? Was his grandad, who always had time to listen to Walter and

make him smile, going crazy? He didn't
want to think so. He didn't want his grandad to change.

Later that night, Walter's mum sat on
the end of his bed, like she did every night,
and read him a story.

'Mum,' Walter said, 'I'm almost ten years
of age. Doesn't it annoy you that you still
have to read to me every night?'

'Walter,' Peggy replied, giving him a
gentle kiss, 'Leonardo da Vinci, Alexander
Graham Bell, Walt Disney – they all
needed help with their reading, all their
lives. I enjoy reading to you. It helps me to
slow down.'

Walter smiled at his mum. Maybe I'll tell
her about Mr Strong and Danny Biggles, he
thought. Maybe now is a good time.

'Yeeeaaaah!' Peggy shouted with excitement, just as Walter was about to open his
mouth. She jumped to her feet and raised
her hands in the air. 'I've just had an idea
for a painting: an electric blue tree, with

pink fish, hanging like apples on canary yellow strings! Better paint it before I forget it.' She gave him a big hug and ran from the room, down the hall and into her studio, like a ferret into a rabbit burrow.

Walter sighed. He felt like calling after her but he was too tired and weary. He leaned over to grab his telescope which sat on the table beside the bed. He pointed it through the skylight at the grapefruit-coloured moon over Nittiburg Hill. Its craters looked so close, he was afraid that he might fall in.

5

Danny Biggles gets up his own Nose

Danny Biggles was sitting directly behind Levon Allen. When Mr Strong turned to write on the blackboard, Danny saw a chance to bully Levon. 'Hey, Hoppedy Foureyes, how about a race?' he hissed. Levon had a slight limp as the result of an accident, and Danny never missed an opportunity to taunt him about it. 'I'll tie my feet together and wear a blindfold and I'll still win.'

Levon ignored him.

Then Danny jumped up, ran over, grabbed Levon's glasses from his face and returned quickly to his seat.

Mr Strong turned around to face the class. As always, he had an angry, unhappy look on his face. Then, as he did before every class, he placed his hand on the desk covered in the heavy black material and, for an instant, a look of calm crossed his face. 'OK, Levon Allen, read what's on the blackboard.'

'I can't, sir. I left my glasses at home,' said Levon nervously. He was too scared to tell Mr Strong what had really happened.

'Outside the door, Levon,' shouted Mr Strong, as the calm disappeared from his brow and the familiar furrows reappeared, 'and take your good-for-nothing friend, Speazlebud, with you.'

'What did I do, sir?' asked Walter who was sitting quietly at the back of the class.

'You tore my good blue shirt, Speazlebud – remember?'

'Welcome to the corridor of dreams,' quipped Walter once they were outside the door. 'I like to be out here during reading,' he continued, 'because when I try to read, it's like you trying to read without glasses.'

'You mean you have bad eyesight too, Walter? Why don't you get glasses?'

'Aha,' said Walter, 'my eyesight's fine, but the words look a bit backwards and upside down.'

'But what about tests, Walter? I've seen you read whole chapters.'

'If there's a test coming up, I get my mum to read the chapter to me the night before and I remember every word. I just turn the pages to make it look good.'

'You remember every word? Wow!'

'I'm a bit like my grandad. He has over five hundred books in his room. Every day Nurse Hatchett reads to him for an hour. He knows every book off by heart and every word backwards.'

'He's a backwards wizard!' Levon said excitedly.

Walter froze as if he had just seen an angel land on Levon's head with a bag full of sweets. He looked up and down the corridor. 'Can you keep a secret, Levon? A big, big secret the size of a **tnahpele**?'

Levon's eyes lit up like fireflies in the night. Being Walter's friend, he knew enough backwards spelling to understand that a secret as big as a **tnahpele** was about as big as secrets can possibly get.

'OK,' he said.

'Well, you see,' said Walter very quietly, while looking around for nosey parkers, 'he *may be* some kind of wizard. He says he has the power of **Noitanigami**, whatever that is ... or else *he may be going crazy*. I'm just not sure.'

'Walter,' said Levon. 'That magic stuff only happens in books. I know you wish he was a wizard, and so do I, because then he could help us with our problems – with Biggles and Strong.'

'You're right, Levon. I'm just dreaming as usual.'

The bell rang. Danny Biggles came out of the classroom and dropped Levon's glasses on the ground.

'I found these in my pocket, Hoppedy.

Better pick 'em up before someone steps on 'em.'

Then Danny stuck a finger right up his left nostril until he could feel his eyeball from behind. He moved his bulging eyeball from side to side, and up and down, and he looked like a monster from a medieval swamp. Walter and Levon felt sick.

Danny slowly pulled his finger out and wiped his putrid, slimy snot across Walter's shirt. 'You're next, boy,' he said with a grisly laugh.

'I wish I could make that disgusting bully go backwards out of our lives,' Walter said, wiping the green yuck from his shirt when Danny had left.

'Not half as much as I do,' replied Levon. 'Not half as much as I do.'

After school that day, when everybody had gone home, Danny Biggles sneaked back into the classroom and wrote in large letters on the blackboard, '**RM GNORTS SI A GIB LOOLF**.'

6

The Cat goes 'Zipp'

Walter's kitchen was red with yellow pin-
stripes. The lampshade was leopard-skin,
and the toaster, microwave and refriger-
ator were covered in vibrant pink fur.
When he arrived home, he plonked himself
on the big Dalmatian, the spotted arm-
chair. He was in a *very* bad mood again. Mr
Strong was as horrible as ever, Danny
Biggles was being a rotten bully, his
parents were too busy to listen to his
troubles, and Grandad Speazlebud was
getting older in front of his eyes and possibly going simple in the head. Could
things get much worse? he thought. He saw
a note on the table which said:

Suoitpmurcs hsif rennid ni eht rotaregirfer.
Owt setunim ni eht evaworcim dluohs od ti.

F.vol Mum

(Scrumptious fish dinner in the refriger-
ator. Two minutes in the microwave should
do it.
Love Mum)

Walter was starving. Maybe he would
feel a little better after a big feed. He
certainly couldn't feel any worse.

As Walter walked towards the refriger-
ator, he noticed that the door was ajar.
When he looked inside he saw, to his
horror, instead of a delicious fish dinner, an
empty plate covered in hairs that looked
suspiciously like the hairs of a ginger cat.

On top of the food cupboard, above the
sink, Walter spotted a bushy ginger tail,
quivering.

'**Ajaraham**!' Walter shouted in a rage,
but Maharaja stuck to his hiding place.
'**Ajaraham**!' he shouted again. Just as he
said the third '**Ajaraham**!', Maharaja shot
out from behind the cupboard, leaped backwards onto the floor, reversed out through
the cat flap, across the lawn, and up into
the top branches of the beech tree.

Walter was highly surprised. What a strange thing, he thought. Maybe **Ajaraham** is going a bit crazy, like Grandad. He reached into the fridge to take out some cheese. Then he froze, as he remembered his favourite story. Grandad's voice echoed in his head:

'Without thinking, I shouted the word "deer" backwards, again and again. "**Reed! Reed! Reed!**" On the third "**reed**", the deer zipped backwards across the road and into the forest, safe from the fast-approaching car.'

'Grandad!' Walter shouted, unable to contain his excitement, 'You're not crazy after all! There is such a thing as **Noitanigami!**'

Walter opened the door and cartwheeled across the lawn, climbed the beech tree and took a slightly dazed Maharaja in his arms, like a rocket scientist might hold a monkey who had returned to earth after circling the Earth for five years.

Carrying Maharaja, Walter went back inside, put the cat in his basket and phoned Levon. 'Levon, it's Walter.'

'Hi, Walter. You sound like you're out of breath.'

'I have it!' Walter said.

'Have what, Walter?'

'The power of **Noitanigami**, just like Grandad.'

'Wow!' said Levon. 'My best friend is a wizard. Tell me again. What is **Noitanigami** exactly? What can you do?'

Through the kitchen window Walter could see his dad driving the loomobile around the garden, steering with one hand, his other hand raised in a victory salute.

'It's working perfectly. It's finished!' Harry shouted through the open window. 'I'm going to be a millionaire.' With that, Harry fell, backwards, into the toilet as the loomobile went wildly out of control.

'Gotta run, Levon,' said Walter. 'Emergency.'

Walter dashed outside, just as his dad and the loomobile crashed into the privet hedge. The passenger door fell off, and all

that Walter could see were two highly
polished shoes and a pair of hands sticking
out of the toilet. Walter tried desperately to
pull his dad free. Maharaja picked that
moment to arrive to inspect the scene. The
oversized ginger cat hopped onto Walter's
shoulder and then onto the flusher bar,
sticking out of the roof of the loomobile.

'Maharaja!' yelled Walter. But it was too
late. The loomobile flushed with a rushing,
slurping sound, and Harry Speazlebud's
hands and feet disappeared. Walter knew
that he had to try his new powers in a
hurry.

'**Yrrah Dubelzaeps! Yrrah Dubelzaeps! Yrrah Dubelzaeps!**' he said, while
shooing Maharaja away with his hands.
With that, Maharaja zipped, once again,
backwards, up onto the flusher, onto Walter's shoulder, across the lawn, through the
cat flap and back into his basket.

Oops, he said to himself. Maybe I should
be thinking of Dad and not the cat while I
say the spell. I'll try it once again. Oh, and

I mustn't forget to phone Levon back. Wait until he hears about this!

Walter tried once more: '**Yrrah Dubelzaeps! Yrrah Dubelzaeps! Yrrah Dubelzaeps!**'

Levon was nodding off in front of the TV when suddenly he found himself back by the telephone where he had been moments earlier, talking to Walter.

'I've never sleep-walked before,' he said to himself. 'That's the oddest thing.'

Back at Walter's house, his dad was still down the toilet.

'I'll have to try and concentrate harder,' Walter said, becoming very frustrated.

'**Yrrah Dubelzaeps! Yrrah Dubelzaeps! Yrrah Dubelzaeps!**' he said, this time picturing his dad very clearly in his mind.

It worked! His dad popped out of the toilet, dripping wet, and back onto the seat, gasping for air.

Walter breathed a sigh of relief. 'Still a bit of work to do on the loomobile, Dad,' he said, with a smile.

'The problem seems to be that the seat is just a little bit too wide, Walter. Just that little bit too wide.' Then, still dripping with water, he began measuring the toilet seat. 'That flusher needs looking at too,' continued Harry, as he shook his head like a shaggy dog that had just come in from a rainstorm.

7

Mr Strong goes Crazy

Mr Strong arrived in the classroom at eight o'clock. Summer exams were just around the corner and he loved to come in early to write questions. It was the best time of the day for clear thinking, he believed, the best time of the day to think up the most difficult questions of all. When he saw the writing on the blackboard, he scratched his head. It was just gobbledegook as far as he could see – probably the Russian cleaning lady writing down the day's chores.

He sat down at his desk and, checking to see that nobody was peeping in the window, he placed both his hands on the desk's thick black covering. He closed his eyes and, like a blind man reading Braille, moved his fingers slowly across the desktop.

Just for a moment, Mr Strong seemed to look younger and more alive. Finally, he opened his eyes with a sigh and stood up. He turned and was about to wipe the blackboard when a look of horror flashed over his face. He knew about Walter's talent for spelling backwards. He had seen the boys gather round him in the playground like he was a little pop star, asking him to spell and pronounce their names backwards. 'That boy needs taking down a couple of pegs,' he would hiss to himself underneath his breath at such a moment. Now he suspected that this gobbledegook, **RM GNORTS SI A GIB LOOLF**, which he saw before him, could be the work of his least favourite pupil. He took a piece of chalk and underneath **RM GNORTS** he wrote the letters, **M-R S-T-R-O-N-G**. 'Aha,' he said.

Then he reversed all the other letters, one by one, until he discovered that the full sentence read '**MR STRONG IS A BIG FLOOL**.'

When Walter arrived into class, he found Mr Strong fuming with anger. As he was about to sit down beside Levon, Mr Strong caught Walter by the ear lobe and yanked him from his seat. 'If you think that you can get away with something like this, Walter Speazlebud, you have another thing coming.'

'What, sir?' asked Walter, grimacing with pain.

'Don't "what" me!' said Mr Strong as he spun Walter around to face the blackboard which had '**MR STRONG IS A BIG FLOOL**' written directly under Danny Biggles' writing.

'It wasn't me, sir,' protested Walter. 'I know how to spell the word "fool" backwards. It's only got four letters, sir.'

Walter turned to Danny Biggles. 'Your spelling is almost as bad as mine, Danny.'

Danny gave Walter a drop-dead look.

'Get outside the door until four o'clock,' Mr Strong shouted at Walter. 'I'll put manners on you then.'

Danny Biggles giggled uncontrollably.

Immediately the bell rang, Mr Strong went outside and took Walter by the ear lobe again. 'We'll see what your parents have to say about this,' he said as he dragged Walter down the corridor.

On the way home, Walter saw Mr Spring, the carpet cleaner. 'Hello, Mr **Gnirps**,' he said.

'Hello, **Retlaw**,' Mr Spring called back. '**Ylevol yad**.'

When they arrived at Walter's house, his mum was inside having lunch.

'What a ghastly colour scheme,' Mr Strong mumbled as he rang the doorbell.

When she opened the door, Peggy Speazlebud saw a very unhappy Walter and a fuming Mr Strong.

'Hi, Mum,' said Walter.

'Oh, I see, you didn't say *her* name backwards,' said Mr Strong.

'Oh, but I did,' said Walter. 'I always do.'

But Mr Strong did not believe him.

'What have you done, Walter?' Peggy asked.

'Nothing,' replied Walter.

Before Mr Strong had a chance to say anything else, Sam Silver's truck drew up outside the Speazlebuds' house, with Levon sitting, smiling, in the front seat. A side-door opened, and Sam Silver and his camera crew jumped out and ran across the lawn.

'I'm Sam Silver from ABD News,' said Sam Silver, the grey-haired TV star. 'I'm here to interview the boy-wonder, Walter Speazlebud, or should I say "**Retlaw Dubelzaeps**". That must be you.' Sam reached out to shake Walter's hand.

Mr Strong thought he was seeing things. 'He's an illiterate, trouble-making smarty-pants,' he said under his breath.

Sam turned to the camera.

'Hi, I'm Sam Silver, and you are watching "Most Gifted". I am here to talk to the boy who spells backwards, Walter Speazlebud.'

'I'm Mr Strong, Walter's teacher,' Mr Strong interrupted. 'I'm the one you should be interviewing.'

Sam turned to Mr Strong as Walter, surprised, excited and confused, shook his head. Peggy ducked back inside the house to make peach tea and sweet lemon sandwiches for everybody.

'Indeed, Mr Strong,' said Sam, 'you must deserve a lot of credit for helping Walter to develop his very unusual talent. To be able to develop the imagination and individual gifts of boys like Walter, you must be a very exceptional teacher indeed.'

'Oh, yes,' said Mr Strong in a very insincere tone. 'I like to help my students to develop their talents, no matter how unusual those talents may be.'

Maharaja, who was standing by Walter's side, seemed to be staring at Mr Strong while shaking his head in disbelief.

As people often do when they are telling lies, Mr Strong scratched his nose and then put his hand back down by his side. Suddenly, his hand flew back up and he punched his own nose. 'Ouch!' he shouted, knocking himself backwards. Again it happened, and again. Mr Strong kept on knocking himself sideways and backwards. 'Aeeooow, Uuuhh!'

Sam Silver looked on, completely bemused. All that Mr Strong could do was to pretend that it was an act – a clown act. So he put on a silly face and shouted loudly every time he landed himself a punch.

Walter smiled. He now knew for sure that Grandad Speazlebud was watching, and he was performing TV's first-ever live **Noitanigami**.'

'I see that you're quite the clown,' said Sam Silver, trying to be kind, 'but you are certainly not what we would call "Most Gifted".'

'I'm sorry,' said Mr Strong, recovering from the blows while fearing another at any moment. 'I don't know what I was thinking. Now I must return to school with my prize pupil.'

'Oh, but not before we speak to Walter,' said Sam Silver. 'Walter Speazlebud is this week's "Most Gifted".'

Mr Strong stormed off as Sam turned to face Walter.

'Walter, when did you start to spell backwards?' asked Sam.

'I spend a lot of time outside in the corridor, so that gives me plenty of time to practise.'

'What a funny boy,' said Sam. 'I bet you are the most prized pupil at your school. Now, Walter,' he continued, 'I would like you to spell one word backwards for our millions of viewers: **SUPERCALAFRAGILISTIC-EXPEALIDOCIOUS.**'

Walter didn't even have to stop to think. '**S-U-O-I-C-O-D-I-L-A-E-P-X-E-C-I-T-S-I-L-I-G-A-R-F-A-L-A-C-R-E-P-U-S,**' he rattled off effortlessly.

'Extraordinary!' gushed Sam.

'**Y-R-A-N-I-D-R-O-A-R-T-X-E,**' said Walter.

An engine began to roar in the background. Sam looked to his left and saw the loomobile, out of control, careering around the garden. 'What is that very strange automobile in your garden?' he asked.

'It's the loomobile,' said Walter as he nervously watched his dad trying to bring the loomobile under control. 'Eh, it's my dad's invention.' With that, the loomobile lunged towards the house, missing Sam Silver by centimetres, before plunging into the garden pond in front of ten million viewers.

8

A Chat with Grandad

Walter just had to tell his grandad that he had discovered his own powers of **Noitani-gami**. As he arrived at the nursing home, Grandad spotted him from his upstairs window. 'You're **suomaf, Retlaw**!' he shouted down to Walter. 'My grandson is a **VT rats**, a **suomaf VT rats**, Walter Speazlebud is a TV star, woohoo!'

Walter waved and gave his grandad a big smile. As soon as he stepped through the door, Grandad came motoring down the corridor in his wheelchair with Nurse Hatchett jogging behind, out of breath, and waving a big blanket and a woolly cap.

'Put these on!' she demanded. 'Or you'll catch your death of cold.'

Walter had almost forgotten that he had said he would take Grandad Speazlebud for a walk the next time he visited, but Grandad Speazlebud had not.

'I'm not a child,' protested Grandad, as Nurse Hatchett threw the blanket around him. 'Open the door, Walter. I'm coming through,' he called.

It was a beautiful evening, with the scent of wild garlic and rosemary in the air.

'Grandad,' said Walter, 'I have the power.'

Grandad Speazlebud nodded approvingly. 'Yes, Walter, you have the **tfig fo Noitanigami**. Now I know that, when I go, you will be the keeper of the gift of **Noitanigami**, and that makes me very happy.'

Walter didn't like when Grandad said things like 'when I go'. He had noticed, recently, that when he said, 'Goodbye, Grandad, see you tomorrow,' his grandad would reply, 'God willing,' or 'please God.'

This made Walter agitated. 'Don't say that, Grandad. I don't like it when you say that,' he would say. But as the setting sun threw a golden glow onto his grandad's

face on that cool, late spring evening,
Walter could see more clearly than ever
before the deep furrows that the passage of
time had carved. He reached out and gave
his grandad's hand a gentle squeeze, while
a single tear sparkled in the corner of his
eye.

'You see, Walter,' Grandad said, '**Noitanigami** works like this: If you say the
name of a living thing, or object, backwards, three times, while thinking of it
clearly, it will return to its last position.
But there is more to **Noitanigami** than
this. Much more.'

Grandad put his hand into his pocket
and took out a small black book which had
NOITANIGAMI written on the cover.

'This book has all you need to know
about the power. Use it for your own good,
but remember that **Noitanigami** is most
powerful when it is used for the benefit of
others.'

Walter opened the first page. The text was handwritten, backwards.

NOITANIGAMI
Siht tfig os erar,
Nevig ot uoy,
Nac ekam a noillim smaerd emoc eurt,
Nac pots eht worra-daeh fo emit
Dna dnes ti kcab, rof eeht ro eniht
Ot od eht sgniht ey thgim evah enod
Ot niw eht selttab ey thgim evah now
Ot thgir a gnorw, or ylpmis eb
A ssentiw ot s'nam yrotsih

Nehw nekops htiw eht rewop fo hturt
Taht seltsen ni eht traeh fo htuoy
Siht tfig lliw tsac a gnidnilb thgil ...

Neht yreve nam lliw ylerus ees
Eht rewop fo Imagination

NOITANIGAMI
This gift so rare,
Given to you,
Can make a million dreams come true,
Can stop the arrow-head of time
And send it back, for thee or thine
To do the things ye might have done
To win the battles ye might have won
To right a wrong, or simply be
A witness to man's history

When spoken with the power of truth
That nestles in the heart of youth
This gift will cast a blinding light ...

Then every man will surely see
The power of Noitanigami.

Walter smiled and turned some more pages with headings such as:

Slasrever ni a Yrruh (Reversals in a Hurry)
Levart fo Emit (Travel of Time)

Levart fo Dnim (Travel of Mind)

Woh ot Esrever a Lasrever (How to Reverse a Reversal)

Dliw Serutnevda htiw Imagination (Wild Adventures with Noitanigami)

Step On No Pets (The World of the Palindrome)

'Thanks Grandad,' said Walter, as he closed the book and put it safely in his pocket.

At the bottom of the avenue, Walter and his grandad turned onto Nittiburg Main Street, with its polished cobbles and quaint village air. Grandad saw Mrs Fleming, the florist, and stopped to ask her something. She went inside and returned with a pretty bunch of wild irises. Walter knew that the flowers were for Nurse Hatchett, as Grandad never returned from the village without a gift of some kind.

'I think you like Nurse Hatchett,' Walter teased his grandad.

'I do not,' replied Grandad. 'She's an old bag. I only give her flowers to try and put her off the idea of poisoning my porridge.'

9

Danny Biggles pushes his Luck

The following morning, as Walter walked to school with Levon, he noticed that the shopkeepers who had seen him on TV had changed their shop names to the backwards spellings.

'Levon,' Walter said, 'I'd like to do you a favour for getting me on "Most Gifted".'

'No,' Levon replied. 'It was my way of saying thanks to you for getting my bike back. You're my best friend and I knew how much you wanted to be on TV for your grandad.'

'Well,' continued Walter, 'it's really a favour for both of us.'

'Does it have anything to do with Danny Biggles?'

Walter nodded.

'Then I accept,' Levon said, as he shook Walter's hand with a firm grip.

Walter took the book of **Noitanigami** out of his pocket and quickly read a section.

'What's that?' asked Levon.

'It's the handbook of the art of **Noitanigami**, the power to make things go backwards.'

'So that's what it was! I think I went backwards yesterday, Walter. Were you experimenting or something?'

'I guess you could call it that, Levon. Sorry. I'm still trying to get the hang of it. And I completely forgot to phone you back that time. You wouldn't believe what was happening ...'

Once he arrived in the schoolroom, Walter was surrounded by his classmates. 'Well done, Walter, you're our hero,' they all said – except, of course, for Danny Biggles, who stood against the wall with his arms folded, giving Walter a 'drop-dead' stare.

Walter was not in the least bit scared. 'What's wrong, Danny?' he asked boldly. 'Why don't you run off and play with somebody your own age?'

The boys went silent. Nobody had ever mentioned the age difference to Danny before. Some turned away, afraid to watch what might happen next.

Danny took a run at Walter, knocking him to the ground with the force of his huge frame. He sat on top of Walter. 'I'm going to punch your face in,' he yelled, as he lifted his fist.

'Leave him alone!' cried Levon. 'Leave him alone!'

Walter remained calm and stared into Danny's eyes.

'Ynnad Selggib, Ynnad Selggib, Ynnad Selggib,' he said quickly, as Danny's fist powered towards his face. For a split second Danny was frozen in motion like a photograph, his big fist just two centimetres from Walter's face. Then, like a reverse motion sequence on TV, Danny was propelled backwards, to his feet and out the door. Walter lay on the ground in deep concentration.

The boys looked on aghast. 'I've never seen Danny move so quickly,' said Harry Gordon. Levon smiled at Walter.

Mr Strong arrived into class just as Walter picked himself off the ground. Their teacher looked angry and he spoke with a nasty, sarcastic tone.

'You're very quiet, Walter. Shouldn't you be saying thanks to your teacher for helping you to spell backwards and become famous?'

Walter did not respond.

'Something strange happened yesterday,' Mr Strong continued. 'I suspect that either you were behind it or your grandfather was. I was humiliated in front of millions of people. You will suffer, Walter Speazlebud. I will make your life an unbearable hell. You will wish you *were* living on the moon.'

Just then, Danny Biggles arrived back into class, barely recognisable from the oversized bully-boy who had terrorised Nittiburg School for years. Danny was now two years younger and ten centimetres smaller than he had been just one minute ago. In fact, Danny was now the smallest boy in the class. Yes, he still had all his recognisable features – flat face, flat nose and buck-teeth – but now he seemed shy and awkward. Walter had worked the power of **Noitanigami** on him: he'd reversed him in time for two whole years until he was the same age as everybody else in the class.

'Excuse me, sir,' said the new Danny to Mr Strong, 'may I join your class please? I'm sorry I'm late. It won't happen again.'

Mr Strong was beginning to look nervous. He clasped his hands together to stop his fingers from trembling. 'What's going on here?' he demanded, glancing at this young, gentle Danny Biggles, then at the boys, until his gaze finally settled on Walter. 'Are you behind this dreadful joke, Walter Speazlebud? What is this ... magic

... wizardry ... the dark arts ... just what is going on?'

'It's the power of **Noitanigami**,' Walter replied.

'Noita– what?' shouted Mr Strong, growing increasingly nervous by the second.

'Don't worry, Mr Strong, **Noitanigami** is just the word "imagination" backwards.'

'I always said imagination was a dangerous thing, especially when it gets into the hands of dreamers, like you and your grandfather ...'

'But you were a dreamer once, Mr Strong. Isn't that right? A very talented dreamer.'

'What the hell are you talking about?' growled Mr Strong.

'I'm talking about your talent as a woodcarver and furniture-maker and your dream of becoming one of the world's best furniture-makers.'

'Woodcarving? I'm a teacher, not a bloomin' carpenter,' scoffed Mr Strong.

'Why, then,' asked Walter, walking

towards the top of the class, 'do you have your desk covered with this thick piece of cloth?'

'Stay away from that desk, Walter Speazlebud, or you will be expelled from this school!'

Walter didn't seem to care. Swiftly he pulled back the thick, black, felt material from Mr Strong's desk. A cloud of dust, lit by a light beam coming through the window, filled the air. Sticks of coloured chalk, a duster, notebooks, and a large dictionary fell to the floor through the golden dust-cloud, as if in slow motion.

Walter stared at the desktop in amazement – it was completely covered in beautiful hand carvings: roses, their buds bursting into blossom; giant sunflowers, every petal and pollen-grain lovingly carved in microscopic detail; butterflies and bumblebees dipping for nectar; and swallows dive-dancing through the air.

Mr Strong opened his mouth to scream, but nothing came out. He threw his arms

around himself as if it was he who had
been uncovered, and he gazed, with his
mouth still open, upon his past, upon the
fruits of his imagination which had been
hidden for so long by a black felt veil.

Walter's eyes danced and sparkled as he
saw, in every detail, the gifted hand that
worked the wood and the precise eye that
followed the chisel, just as Grandad had
told him. For a moment, Walter wondered
if his own gift – the power of **Noitanigami**
– could, in its own way, be just as beautiful,
just as rich and just as wonderful.

Mr Strong stared at his desk for a
moment, but he could not bear to look.
'Give me that cover, Speazlebud,' he roared,
as he began to chase Walter around the
desk.

But Walter was too quick. 'My grandfather told me that you were a most gifted
woodcarver and furniture-maker,' he said,
as he continued to dart around the table,
avoiding Mr Strong. 'You could have
become one of the best.'

'Stop! Stop! Stop!' shouted Mr Strong, as he ran out of breath and rested his hands on the desk. 'I'm a teacher, not a carpenter. I'm a teacher.'

'You're *not* a teacher, Mr Strong, and you know it. You were never meant to be a teacher – it was not your gift.'

Mr Strong seemed startled to feel the detail of his own carvings beneath his hands as he rested on the table – detail which, for so long, he had felt only through the material. His face lost its anger as he studied the flowers and insects which he had created with his own hands. Tears welled up in his eyes. Then he covered his face with his hands and fell over onto the carved desktop – a broken man – disappointed in himself and his sad, angry life.

Walter and the class heard a muffled sob. 'You're right,' he cried. 'I'm not a teacher. I never wanted to be a teacher. I should never have been a teacher. I wanted to be a woodcarver. I wanted to be a woodcarver!'

Mr Strong wiped his tears as he stood up again and turned towards the door. He took his grey mac from behind his chair and walked out of the classroom for the very last time.

Walter was surprised to feel sadness, as well as joy, as he sat, for a moment, in Mr Strong's chair. He thought of something that his grandfather had said. He took his little black book from his pocket, opened it and read some more. Then he concentrated deeply.

10

A Second Chance

Walter walked up Runyon Hill. His steps
were quick. He was a boy on a mission,
with a sparkle in his eye. As he neared the
gates of the nursing home, he saw a teenager coming towards him. He was a handsome boy, around eighteen, with a kind
face and bright green eyes. The young man
had a pep in his step and a warm glow
about him. 'Can you tell me what time the
next train leaves for the city?' he asked
politely.

'I believe it's every two hours,' replied
Walter. 'Are you going to the city for the day?'

'I'm off to the city to live,' the boy replied
happily. 'I'm going to become a furniture-
maker and woodcarver.'

Walter smiled. It had worked, he
thought. It had actually worked brilliantly.

Walter shook the hand of Frank Strong and wished him all the luck in the world.

'What's your name?' asked the teenager.

'Walter, Walter Speazlebud.'

'You must be related to Mr Speazlebud the carpenter.'

'Yes, he's my grandfather.'

'What a lucky boy you are to have him as your grandfather.'

'I know,' said Walter. 'I'm the luckiest boy alive.'

As Walter walked through the gates of the nursing home, he was struck by a blinding orange light. He thought for a moment that he had accidentally walked in through the gates of a nightmare. Nittiburg Nursing Home was now the same colour as his own house – 'exploding orange' with green polka dots and purple window frames. Slowly, and with a sense of dread, he turned and looked down over the village. Luminous pink, bile green, day-glow red and 'exploding orange' houses dotted the landscape. It seemed that Sam Silver's TV show had made his mum's house-painting famous, and now everybody wanted a vibrant, clashing colour scheme just like theirs.

Walter climbed the stairs and walked down the corridor to his grandad's room. The old people sitting in the corridor now called out to him, 'Walter, well done! We saw you on TV. You're a chip off the old block, that's for sure!'

When he entered Grandad's room, he found it was empty. 'Grandad!' Walter shouted in a panic, as he ran out into the hall, 'Grandad!'

Around the corner appeared a dapper little old man in a wheelchair; he was wearing a smart, beige summer suit and a Panama hat with a golden-brown feather.

'Have you seen my grandad?' asked Walter frantically.

The old man smiled. 'Walter,' he said, with a youthful smile, 'you're certainly learning fast.'

Walter realised that the dapper old man with the big beaming smile *was* his grandad!

'You have given me a most wonderful surprise. I never thought I'd see Frank Strong again. I'm so happy. I decided to dress up in my favourite suit to celebrate.'

'When Mr Strong left the class,' Walter said, 'I thought about how you had said that one of your biggest regrets was not being able to convince him to follow his dream. So I thought I'd give you a second chance.'

'Frank Strong was certainly happy when he left here, so you gave him a second chance too,' said Grandad.

'Well,' said Walter, 'as the saying goes, "It's never too late to be what you might have been."'

Nurse Hatchett popped her head around the corner. 'He looks so handsome, doesn't he, Walter?' she said as she flashed her eyelids.

Grandad gave Walter a wink.

'He looks like a Hollywood star, Nurse Hatchett,' replied Walter, with a grin.

'Don't forget to take some blankets if you're going outside,' said Nurse Hatchett.

'It's almost summer, Nurse Hatchett. Relax,' said Grandad, in his best movie-star voice.

'Frank Strong was a bit confused at first,' Grandad said, as he and Walter went down the hall together. 'He hadn't seen me for almost thirty-five years. He said that he wanted to become my apprentice, but I explained that I retired from carpentry and woodcarving twenty years ago! I sent him to one of the top furniture-makers in the city.'

They stopped by the large window on the second-floor landing.

'Is he going to take the Condor Chair away?' asked Walter.

'I did offer to return it to him,' Grandad replied. 'But he said he wouldn't dream of it. Of course, I will leave it to you when I go.'

'Go where?' asked Walter.

There was a moment's silence, which seemed to last an eternity.

'When I die,' Grandad replied gently.

'Grandad,' Walter said excitedly, reaching out to grasp the old man's hand. 'That is why I have come to see you. I have this great idea!' Walter looked around to check for nosey parkers.

'I want to use the power of **Noitanigami** to make you younger, so that you can drink tea without spilling it, and make furniture again, and come back to live with Dad and Mum and me.'

'Walter,' Grandad said quietly. 'I have been on this planet for over eighty wonderful years, and I have lived every day as if it might be the last. Yes, I am coming to the end of my days. It may be tomorrow, it may be next year, or the year after, but when it is time, it is time. I have led a long and happy life and that's all I ever wished and hoped for.'

'But wouldn't you like to stay here longer so that we can spend more time together?' Walter asked, a little sadly.

'Walter,' Grandad replied, 'although I

love you dearly, I cannot ask for a second more than I am given in this life.'

'Do you see that setting sun?' he continued, pointing to the hazy orange sun throwing a warm glow over the village. 'Should we call it back and tell the moon to wait?'

Walter thought about it. 'I suppose not. It wouldn't seem right, would it? Besides,' he added, with a slight smirk, 'I love the moon.' Then a big smile broke out on his freckly face. 'But I love my grandad even more,' he said, as he gave Grandad a huge hug.

'What are we doing here?' said Grandad, all flustered but looking very chuffed. 'I'm dressed for going out. Let's go watch that sunset.'

11

Off to the Moon

Together they ambled down Runyon Hill, chatting as they went, with swallows dancing over their heads and at their feet. They stopped at the bench overlooking the village.

'Did I ever tell you how I tidied up this town, Walter?' asked Grandad.

'No,' replied Walter, 'but I reckoned it was by good example – always putting your wrappers and apple cores in the bin.'

'Indeed,' said Grandad. 'But sometimes good example is not enough.'

'What do you mean?' asked Walter.

'Well,' said Grandad, 'Nittiburg's name as the tidiest village in the land is all down to … **Noitanigami**.'

Walter stopped and looked for a trace of a smile on his grandad's face, but Grandad looked very serious indeed.

'On my very first evening as Mayor of Nittiburg,' he began, 'I simply said the word "rubbish" backwards – **hsibbur** – three times, while in my mind's eye I imagined all the sweet wrappers, cigarette butts, crisp bags and chewing gum returning to their rightful owners.

'On that evening, our Mr Strong was giving a talk at the parent–teacher meeting in the school when two sweet wrappers, a large apple core and a piece of dirty chewing gum rolled in the door. When Mr Strong saw the litter coming, he stopped talking and ran, but the litter chased him around the hall until it finally caught up with him. The wrappers and the apple core jumped straight into his pocket, while the dirty chewing gum shot right back into his mouth. He always suspected I had something to do with it as he'd heard me spell and sing backwards in my workshop. There was no littering in Nittiburg from that day onwards,' said Grandad, smiling.

Walter snorted with laughter. 'That's my

new favourite story, Grandad,' he said.

Then they heard the sound of joyous shouting coming from a house down the hill.

'Why is that person laughing?' asked Grandad. 'Is my voice really that loud, Walter?'

'That's Dad down there in the garden,' Walter explained, grinning. 'He's working on his new invention – the pedal-dryer, a bike with a compartment for drying clothes. At least it's more environmentally friendly than the loomobile!'

Grandad chuckled, 'So, the loomobile went down the toilet?'

'Actually, it's still in the pond,' replied Walter, pointing towards the house with a smile. 'Grandad,' he continued, 'I was wondering ...'

'What were you wondering, Walter?'

'I was wondering if you'll marry Nurse Hatchett?'

Grandad looked at Walter. 'You do have a wild imagination, Walter, don't you? Boy, you do have a wild imagination.'

'And so do you, Grandad,' Walter said.

Grandad and Walter watched, content-
edly, as the sun disappeared and the moon
rose slowly over the horizon.

'That's where I'm going to live in the
future,' said Walter, pointing at the now
full moon.

'Wouldn't you miss this wonderful planet
of ours?' asked Grandad.

'Well, with **Noitanigami**,' said Walter, 'I
can always come back if I need to.'

'I forgot to tell you, Walter,' Grandad
said, 'you can't perform **Noitanigami** on
yourself.'

'Then you're going to have to stay
around, Grandad, in case I need you to
bring me home. You'll just have to stick
around for a long, long time.'

A Note from the Author

Hi, Readers!

When I was around ten or eleven, I discovered that I could spell backwards – any word – just as fast as anybody else could spell forwards. I had developed the talent during the hours and hours I spent standing, dreaming, in the corridor of the CBS Primary School in Carlow, mainly for being a 'cheeky pup' and answering back.

School bored me silly, or, more precisely, boring teachers bored me – teachers who, like Mr Strong, should really have been doing something else with their lives, like fishing for electric eels with metal fishing rods, digging holes with their bare hands, or running for Taoiseach in their bare feet, on a gravel road – whatever, but not teaching, nooooooooo.

Anyway, for years I wondered why my wonderful gift could not be used to make a few shillings, pounds, euro. When I was in my twenties (I'm 41 now, or 14 backwards, which is probably closer to the truth) and lived in New York, I even tried to get a job once as a backwards speller in a weird talent show, alongside people who ate worms and drank cider through their noses, but they turned me down.

Later, having written several children's stories which 'nearly' got published, a friend suggested that I write about something that came from my own experience. *Walter Speazlebud* is that story. But apart from being about spelling backwards and school, this story is also about the gift of having people: family, friends, teachers (yes, there are many GREAT teachers out there), who can encourage you and inspire you to follow your dreams and, most importantly, to use your **Noitanigami**.

I've done quite a few different things in my life, but writing this story has been one of the most enjoyable and rewarding things I've ever done. I hope you have enjoyed it, and if you ever have any big words you need spelt backwards, I'm your man ...

Ekat erac

David Donohue

VISIT
www.obrien.ie
website

What's on www.obrien.ie?

➤ detailed information on *all* O'Brien Press
books, both current and forthcoming

➤ sample chapters from many books

➤ author information

➤ book reviews by other readers

➤ authors writing about their own books

➤ teachers' and students' thoughts about
author visits to their schools

What are you waiting for?
Check out <u>www.obrien.ie</u> today.